The Time Machine

Retold from the H.G. Wells original
by Chris Sasaki

Illustrated by Troy Howell

STERLING CHILDREN'S BOOKS
New York

STERLING CHILDREN'S BOOKS
New York

An Imprint of Sterling Publishing
387 Park Avenue South
New York, NY 10016

STERLING CHILDREN'S BOOKS and the distinctive Sterling Children's Books logo are trademarks of Sterling Publishing Co., Inc.

Classic Starts is a trademark of Sterling Publishing Co., Inc.

ISBN 978-1-4027-4582-9

Library of Congress Cataloging-in-Publication Data

Sasaki, Chris.
 The time machine / retold from the H.G. Wells original; abridged by
Chris Sasaki; illustrated by Troy Howell; afterword by Arthur Pober.
    p. cm. —- (Classic starts)
 Summary: An abridged version of the science fiction novel about the scientist who invents a time machine and uses it to travel to the year 802,701 A.D., where he discovers the childlike Eloi and the hideous underground Morlocks.
 ISBN 978-1-4027-4582-9
 [1. Time travel—Fiction. 2. Science fiction.] I. Howell, Troy, ill. II. Wells, H. G. (Herbert George), 1866–1946. Time machine. III. Title.

PZ7.S24864Ti 2008
[Fic]—dc22

2007004482

Distributed in Canada by Sterling Publishing
c/o Canadian Manda Group, 165 Dufferin Street,
Toronto, Ontario, Canada M6K 3H6
Distributed in the United Kingdom by GMC Distribution Services,
Castle Place, 166 High Street, Lewes, East Sussex, England BN7 1XU
Distributed in Australia by Capricorn Link (Australia) Pty. Ltd.
P.O. Box 704, Windsor, NSW 2756, Australia

For information about custom editions, special sales, and premium and corporate purchases, please contact Sterling Special Sales at 800-805-5489 or specialsales@sterlingpublishing.com.

Printed in China
Lot#:
10 9
08/16

CONTENTS

᭜

CHAPTER 1:

The Time Traveler 1

CHAPTER 2:

The Time Traveler's Surprise 15

CHAPTER 3:

The Time Traveler's Story—
in His Own Words 21

CHAPTER 4:

The Eloi 31

CHAPTER 5:

Paradise 38

CHAPTER 6:

The Disappearance of the Time Machine 45

CHAPTER 7:

More Discoveries 52

CHAPTER 8:

Weena 57

CHAPTER 9:

Encounter with a Ghost 61

CHAPTER 10:

A Visit to the Underworld 70

CHAPTER 11:

To the Green Building 80

CHAPTER 12:

The Museum 89

CHAPTER 13:

The Forest at Night 100

CHAPTER 14:

Recovering the Time Machine 112

CHAPTER 15:

Into the Future Again 119

CHAPTER 16:

The Time Traveler Returns 130

CHAPTER 17:

The Proof 133

Epilogue 140

What Do *You* Think? 143
Afterword 147
Classic Starts™ Library 152

CHAPTER 1

The Time Traveler

I will call my friend the Time Traveler. It was Thursday, and I was on my way to his house. He had invited me to dinner, and it was such a lovely evening that I decided to walk. The streets of London were busy with people enjoying the night. Horse-drawn carriages rattled by. The flickering flames of streetlamps began to light my way.

As I crossed the River Thames, I saw the last rays of the setting sun reflected in the water. By the time I arrived at the Time Traveler's home, it was night. My friend Filby was there, along with the mayor, the doctor, and the artist.

After a wonderful meal, we moved to the study. The fire in the fireplace and the burning lamps and candles made the room glow. The lights of the city shone through the windows. Our friend the Time Traveler was an inventor. Some of the odd devices he had made were scattered on the shelves and tables around us. Once we all sat down, he began to speak, his gray eyes twinkling and his face red with excitement.

"Listen carefully," he said, moving his hands about as he talked. "What I'm going to describe will sound very strange to you. You will probably have a hard time believing me. The reason it will sound far-fetched is because it means that much of what you were taught in school was wrong."

"That does sound strange," said Filby.

"I know," said the Time Traveler. "But let me explain."

He paused, took a breath, and continued. "Now, we've all been taught that every object has three *dimensions*—length, width, and height. For example, that box sitting on the table is about six inches long, four inches wide, and two inches high."

"That's right," said the artist slowly, looking puzzled.

"And you would say that the box has three dimensions and no more. After all, what is there besides length, width, and height? Correct?" The Time Traveler paused and looked around the room. "Well, you would be wrong. What they don't teach in you school is that everything also has a *fourth* dimension. And without that fourth dimension, nothing would exist."

"I don't understand," Filby interrupted. "The

box only has three dimensions—and there it is as plain as the nose on my face."

"But wait," said our friend. "I built that box in my workshop a year ago. What if I threw it in the fireplace this very moment and it burned to ashes? We would say that the box existed for one year. And what if I had burned it after only a day? Then we would say that the box had existed for one day. Even if I destroyed the box after one second, we would say that the box existed—for that one second."

"I think I follow," said the mayor.

The Time Traveler leaned forward. "But what if the box didn't last for even a second? What if it didn't last for any time at all? Would we say that it was real, that it ever existed?

"Clearly," said the Time Traveler, "the box must exist in *four* dimensions to be real. It must have length, width, height—*and* it must exist in *time*. Time is the fourth dimension. And there is no difference between time and the other three dimensions."

"But even if time is a dimension, there is a difference," said the doctor. "I can move to my left and right. I can move backward and forward. And I can move up and down. But I can't move through time."

"But you *can* move through time," said our friend with great excitement. "For one thing, we are always moving forward through time—from the moment we are born to the day we die."

"Yes, but with the other three dimensions, I can move in both directions," said the artist. "I can't move backward and forward in time."

"But that is where you are wrong," said the Time Traveler. "We move left and right or back and forth with the help of our legs, or a boat, or a carriage. We can move up and down with the help of stairs, a ladder, or a hot-air balloon.

"And, with the right means, I say we *can* go

5

back and forth through time. I say we can go slowly or quickly. We can even stop and change direction."

"Oh, this doesn't make any sense at all," argued Filby.

"What if there was a machine that could travel through *time* the way other machines travel through the other dimensions?" the Time Traveler asked.

"That would be wonderful!" said the artist. "You could travel back through time and see all of history. You could witness the great events that you only read about in history books. Imagine meeting Napoleon or Christopher Columbus!"

"And you could travel into the future," said the mayor. "You could put all your money in the bank, then travel thousands of years from today. When you arrived, you'd find your savings had grown into a fortune!"

"Yes," said the doctor, chuckling. "Or you might find yourself in a future where people no longer use money."

"Traveling through time! Of all the wild ideas," said the mayor.

"That's what I thought at first," said the Time Traveler. "Then I began to think about how to build a machine that could cross the ages. I've been working on the problem for years, but I never said anything to any of you. I didn't want to talk about it until I could show you that it worked."

"What!? You've built a Time Machine?" I cried.

The Time Traveler smiled at us, then stood up and left the room. Through the open door we saw him walk down the hall to the workshop where he built his inventions. He disappeared into the room, but was gone for only a minute before he returned.

Our friend stood in the middle of the study holding an odd-looking machine in his hands. It was about the size of a small clock and looked very delicate. Most of the machine was metal, but it also had small parts made of ivory and glimmering crystals. He placed it on a table and pulled the table closer to the fire. We all drew our chairs in to get a good look.

The Time Traveler sat in his chair, looked at us, and then turned to the machine. "This," he began, "is only a model. I built it to test my ideas.

"Do you see this lever?" he asked, pointing to a small part of the machine. "If I push it forward, it will send the machine into the future. If I pull it back, it will send the machine into the past."

Then he pointed to what looked like a tiny chair in the middle of the machine. "And this is where the time traveler will sit.

"In a moment, I am going to push the lever forward. The machine will disappear and travel into the future. I want you all to watch carefully, because you'll only see it once."

After a moment of silence, the Time Traveler moved his hand toward the lever. Then he stopped. "No, one of you should do it—to see that I'm not playing a trick." He looked at the artist and asked, "Would you do the honors?"

The artist turned to us with a surprised look on his face. He gazed down at the machine and slowly reached out his hand. He gently touched the lever with one finger, then pushed it forward. A small breeze blew out one of the candles and made the lamps flicker. The little machine appeared to move. Then it became harder to see. It was disappearing. For a moment, you could see through it, as if it was a ghost. Then it was gone!

No one said a word. The Time Traveler laughed as the mayor looked under the table. We all stared at one another, wide-eyed.

"Look here," the doctor said finally. "You don't expect us to believe your machine has traveled into the future, do you?"

"Yes!" said the Time Traveler with a smile. "Well, the future or the past. I designed it to go forward in time when you push the lever forward, but I can't be certain it works that way. After all, no one has ever built a Time Machine before! But whether it's speeding into the future or the past, I assure you that it *is* traveling through time."

"It must have gone into the past," said the mayor.

"What makes you say that?" asked the Time Traveler.

"Well, suppose it traveled an hour into the future—to eleven o'clock," replied the mayor, looking at his watch. "It would still be on the table. To go from ten o'clock—now—to eleven o'clock, it would have to travel *through* one minute past ten. Then it would travel through two minutes past ten, and so on. So it should still be visible on the table."

"That makes sense," muttered the doctor.

"Not at all," said the Time Traveler. "I think it's invisible to us as it travels. It's like the spokes on a spinning bicycle wheel, or a bullet flying through the air. They're moving so fast, we can't see them." He passed his hand over the table where the Time Machine had been sitting and laughed. He was excited at his success.

"Besides," I said, "if it went into the past, it would have been here on this table before we entered the room."

"Unless it went far back in time," replied the doctor. "It might've gone back to the time of the dinosaurs and been crushed beneath their feet millions of years ago."

"I'm glad to see you find the idea so fascinating," the Time Traveler said with a grin. "Because there's more. What you saw was only a small model. I've almost finished building the real thing. And when it's done, I'll use it to carry *me* through time. Would you like to see it?"

We said yes, and the Time Traveler led us down the hallway to his workshop. There, in a corner lit by lamplight, was another machine. It looked like the small model, but it was much bigger. Like the model, it too was made of metal, ivory, and crystal. And like the model, it looked like an odd mix of bicycle, clock, carriage, and radio. We could see that it was almost finished, except for some pieces sitting on the Time Traveler's workbench. Drawings of the machine were scattered around the room.

13

"Look here," said the doctor. "Are you serious, or is this all a trick——a joke?"

"I have never been more serious," said our friend. "With this machine, I intend to leave the year 1895——and explore the depths of time."

CHAPTER 2

The Time Traveler's Surprise

⌒

A week after that curious visit, I received a note from the Time Traveler inviting me to dinner again. The note said he would have another interesting story to tell. When I arrived at his home, the doctor and artist were already there. The mayor and Filby were missing, but two new guests had taken their place. There was the editor of a local newspaper, and a writer. The Time Traveler had invited us all to dinner, but he had not shown up yet.

The doctor pulled a note from his pocket. "Our friend says we should start dinner without him if he is late. It would be a shame to let our meal get cold, don't you think?"

So we went to the dining room, where our friend's housekeeper served us our meal. As we ate, we wondered where our host could be. I joked that he must be busy traveling through time. The editor didn't understand what I meant, so we described the events of the other night.

Just then, the door from the hallway slowly opened. "Here he is at last," I said as the Time Traveler entered the room.

The doctor looked up and cried, "Good heavens, man! What's the matter?"

Our friend was a shocking sight. His coat was dusty and dirty. His hair was a great mess, and it seemed grayer. His face was pale, his chin was cut, and he looked very tired. We stared at him in silence as he stood in the doorway. Then he closed the door and walked to the table. His feet must have been sore or hurt, because he limped as he crossed the floor.

The Time Traveler slumped into a chair. He weakly lifted his hand toward a pitcher of water. The editor filled a glass and handed it to him. Our friend drank the water in one gulp. Then he looked around the table and smiled.

"What on earth have you been up to?" asked the doctor.

The Time Traveler did not answer. Instead, he said in a whisper, "Don't let me disturb you. I'm all right." He held out the water glass and the editor filled it again. After emptying the glass once more, the Time Traveler's eyes seemed to brighten. He looked around the room at each of us as if he'd been away a long time. "I'm going to wash and change my clothes," he said quietly. "Then I'll come down and explain things. Save me some dinner. I'm starving . . ."

He put down his glass and walked to the doorway. It was then I saw that he wasn't wearing shoes on his feet, just ragged socks.

After he left the room, we slowly returned to our meal. The writer was the first to ask, "Just what is going on?"

I said that it must have something to do with the Time Machine, and we explained more about the model and how it had disappeared. The editor and writer thought we were joking.

We continued to talk until the Time Traveler returned. He had washed and was dressed in evening clothes. But our friend still looked very tired, as if he had been through an enormous adventure.

"I say," said the editor with a laugh. "Your friends here say you took a little trip into the middle of next week! Tell us all about it, will you?"

The Time Traveler sat down. He smiled and

said, "What's for dinner? It will be wonderful to have a home-cooked meal again."

"But tell us what happened!" said the editor.

"Not until I've eaten something and gotten my strength back," said our hungry host.

"I must ask one question," I said. "Have you been time traveling?"

Our friend nodded his head and quietly said, "Yes."

We all wanted to hear what had happened, but we had to wait while he finished his meal. We tried to talk about other things, but no one was really interested.

Finally the Time Traveler pushed his empty plate away and looked at us. "I'm sorry," he said. "I've never been hungrier. But now, let's go into the study and I will tell you all about my adventure."

Once we were seated in the next room, the

Time Traveler looked around at us and began. "Since this morning, I have lived through eight days—eight amazing days. I'm worn out, but I can't sleep until I've told you everything. But please, don't interrupt. And please don't tell me you don't believe me, or that it is impossible. Every word I say is true.

"So, no interruptions! Is it agreed?"

"Agreed," we all said. Our weary host then sat back in his chair. The room was dark except for the light from a lamp on the table. I glanced at the others as the Time Traveler began. But as I listened to his tale unfold, I could only look into his pale, white face.

CHAPTER 3

The Time Traveler's Story— in His Own Words

ᥩᥩ

Last Thursday, I told some of you about time travel. And I showed you the machine I was building. It's still in my workroom. But it's been knocked about since last week. One of the ivory bars is cracked. A brass rail is bent. But it still works.

When I showed it to you a week ago, it wasn't finished. I thought it would only take me another day or so to complete it. But it turned out that it wasn't ready until this morning at ten o'clock.

I wrote notes inviting each of you to dinner tonight and asked my housekeeper to have them delivered.

Then I went into my workshop. I looked over my machine one last time, climbed in, and sat in the chair.

When I am sitting in my machine, there is a set of dials in front of me that tells me where I am in time and how fast I am traveling. One dial shows days; another, thousands of days; another, millions of days; and another, billions of days. Each has a hand—like the hand of a clock—that counts the days. Beside the dials is the lever for starting the machine.

I have spent years thinking about time travel and working on my invention, but I could still only guess what was about to happen. After all, I was trying to do something that no one had ever done before. I took the lever in one hand and pushed it ever so slightly. Suddenly I felt dizzy, as if I was falling. Right away, I pulled the lever back to its starting position.

I looked around the room. Everything looked exactly the same. Had anything happened? Then I saw the clock sitting on my workbench. I'd climbed into the machine at ten o'clock in the morning—it was now three-thirty in the afternoon! To me, it felt as if only seconds had passed. But to the outside world, five and a half hours had gone by!

I took a deep breath and pushed the lever forward again. There was a thud, and the room became blurry. It was as if I were looking at everything through water. I saw my housekeeper come in and walk to the garden door. She didn't even look at me. It was as if I was invisible. But the strangest sight was how swiftly she was crossing the floor. It took her only a second or two to enter, walk to the other side of the workshop, and leave again.

My Time Machine worked! I was thrilled and pressed the lever as far forward as it would go. Suddenly it was night. Then, just as quickly, the light coming in the windows returned and it was tomorrow. The room grew faint and blurry. Tomorrow night came, then day again, night again, day again. As the days and nights came faster and faster, a humming sound filled my ears. I looked at the dial that measured days. The hand was counting them off like the second hand of a clock counts off seconds.

It's hard to describe time travel. I felt as if I was in a runaway carriage, being tossed back and forth. I was dizzy and felt as if I was about to crash into something.

Days and nights passed in the blink of an eye. At one point, the walls of the workshop disappeared and I could see outside. The house must have been torn down. I could now see the sun flashing across the sky during the day, followed by the moon at night. I saw the moon go from full, to new, to full in only seconds. That was how quickly a month raced by. I also caught a glimpse of the stars as they whirled overhead.

I was traveling faster and faster into the future. Night and day blurred into a deep blue, like the color of the sky at sunset. The sun was flashing by so quickly, it looked like a streak of light across the sky. The moon looked like a fainter streak.

Inside my machine, the dials were spinning around faster and faster. I saw the streak of the sun's path move from low in the sky, to high in the sky, and back in less than a minute. When the path of the sun was high in the sky, it was summer. When it was low in the sky, it was winter. So a single year was passing by in less than a minute. A whole decade was speeding by in less than ten minutes.

As summer and winter came and went, I saw the world go from green to white and back again. I saw trees sprout, grow, and die.

I saw huge buildings rise up, then suddenly disappear. The city grew and changed shape like some great garden. It was as if London were a living thing.

I began to wonder what I would find when I stopped. What would the city be like? What would people be like? Would they be gentle or savage?

And so I began to think about stopping the machine. But then I wondered, what would happen when I came to a halt? I had started my journey in an empty room. And as long as I was moving quickly through time, I wasn't going to hit anything. But what would happen if I stopped in the middle of a large building? Or a tree?

I told myself I would have to stop sooner or later, and so I made up my mind. I grabbed the lever with both hands and pulled hard. I must have done it too quickly, because there was a loud crashing sound. The Time Machine went flying, and I was thrown through the air.

I landed on the soft ground and tumbled to a stop. The machine lay behind me on its side.

It was raining, and I very quickly became wet. When I caught my breath, I thought it was funny that I had traveled all this way through time— and here I was getting soaked in the rain!

I looked around. I seemed to be on a grass lawn in a garden. There were bushes all around me with bright purple flowers. I saw tall plants with strange white flowers that were a foot wide. Other plants were filled with fruit.

I also saw a white stone statue nearby. It reminded me of an Egyptian Sphinx. The statue was part man and part lion. Great wings stretched from the creature's back. It stood on a large base that appeared to be made of bronze. The statue and the base looked very old.

The rain was letting up. The clouds were parting, and I could see blue sky. Sunlight shone through and lit up the countryside. As the mist cleared, huge white buildings with tall towers appeared in the distance.

I hadn't moved from the site of my workshop, but it was as if I was in a strange new land. I didn't recognize anything, and suddenly felt very far from home. I became afraid and began to panic. From where I sat, I could see into my Time Machine as it lay on the ground. I looked at the dials of the machine and couldn't believe my eyes. It was the year eight hundred and two thousand, seven hundred and one! I had traveled more than eight hundred thousand years into the future! The thought of this made me even more afraid. I quickly got to my feet and tried to turn my machine right side up. It was a struggle, but I pushed hard and finally turned it over.

Now that the machine was upright and I could escape quickly, my fear began to disappear. As I calmed down, I became more curious. I wanted to know more about the world around me. After all, my machine had worked. I was in the future.

I noticed a building nearby, and in one of the windows, I saw people! They were wearing flowing robes and looking at me.

Then I heard voices and saw other people coming toward me through the bushes. A small man stepped onto the grass and walked up to me. He was only four feet tall. He wore a purple robe and had a belt around his waist. His legs were bare, and he wore sandals on his feet.

His face was child-like, and he moved gracefully. But he looked very thin, and I could tell he wasn't very strong. I left my machine and walked toward this man of the future.

CHAPTER 4

The Eloi

The man and I looked at each other. He laughed and smiled, and I saw that he was not afraid. He turned to two others behind him. They spoke in a strange but pleasant-sounding language that I did not understand.

Others arrived until there were ten of them standing around me. They seemed to be asking me questions. But I didn't say anything. They spoke in such a whisper and acted like such shy little animals, I thought my voice would scare them.

The first man stepped forward and touched my hand. Soon they were all gently stroking me. It was as if they wanted to make sure I was real.

They crowded around me, but I wasn't afraid. They were like curious children. A small group of them were standing near the Time Machine. They hardly noticed it. But to be safe, I reached into the machine, unscrewed the lever, and put it safely in my pocket. Without the lever, it wouldn't be going anywhere.

I took a closer look at the faces of these people of the future. Their mouths were small, and they had thin, red lips. Their little chins were pointed. They had small ears, and their eyes were large.

Finally I spoke. In a soft voice, I tried to tell them about myself. I pointed to the machine. I tried to explain, by pointing to the sun, that I was from another time. One of them pointed to the sun, too. Then she made a sound like thunder.

I was confused. Was she asking if I had come from the sun in a thunderstorm? I began to think that these creatures were not as advanced as humans of our time. This surprised me. I always imagined that people would become smarter with time. After all, just think how far we have come since we lived in caves. I would have guessed that people from the year eight hundred and two thousand would be far ahead of us in science and art—in every way. But instead, these people thought I had come from the sun. I was filled with disappointment. I felt as if I had built the greatest invention ever, only to discover a disappointing future.

One of the people came toward me, laughing. She handed me a necklace made of beautiful flowers, and I put it around my neck. I had never

seen this type of blossom before. Everyone smiled
and clapped their hands. Then they all darted
into the bushes to gather more flowers. They
threw the flowers at me until there was a pile of
colorful petals at my feet.

Next, they took my hands and led me past the
great statue to a large, white building. It had a
huge doorway made of carved stone. There were

cracks in the doorway and walls that made the building look very old.

More people greeted me inside. They danced around me in their bright, colorful robes and filled the air with laughter that sounded like singing. I felt out of place in my dark, dirty clothes.

We went into a large room with windows of colored glass. The floor was made of white metal, and it was worn where people had walked for so many years. There were tables made of shiny stone. Great piles of fruit sat on the tables. Some of the fruit looked familiar, but some looked very odd.

We sat down on cushions around the tables and began to eat the fruit. I was hungry, so I was glad we were eating. There were about a hundred people in the room. They all watched as I ate my meal.

The room was beautiful, but it looked old. It looked as if no one had taken care of it. Many of the windows were broken, and the curtains were covered with dust. The corners of some of the tables were broken.

After I had eaten, I attempted to learn the language of the people of the future. I held up a piece of fruit and tried to get them to tell me its name. They didn't seem to understand and gave me an odd look or laughed. Finally one of them understood what I was trying to do. He said a word and then pointed to the fruit. I tried repeating it, which made them laugh even more. But I kept at it, and soon I could say the names of some of the fruit, along with a handful of other objects. I even discovered that they called themselves Eloi.

Next, I tried to get them to tell me their word for *eat,* but they didn't understand. They soon became bored and wandered off. In fact, after a while, they went back to their tables and ignored me as if I were just another Eloi.

So I decided I would go outside and take another look at this world of the future.

CHAPTER 5

Paradise

∽

It was evening, and the sun gave everything a warm glow. As I stood on the stairs of the white building and looked out over the countryside, I could see that everything had changed from the world I knew. The Eloi, the buildings, the flowers, and the fruit were all different. Even the River Thames had changed. After hundreds of thousands of years, the great river had altered its course and now took a different route to the ocean.

I decided to walk to a hill about a mile away to

get a better view of the surrounding area. Along the way, I came across a huge pile of metal and stone, overgrown with plants. It was the remains of a large building that had fallen down long ago. It reminded me of the broken glass and stone in the white building I had just come from. I wondered how long before that building turned into a pile of rubble, too.

As I walked, I noticed a number of wells with small roofs over them. But I didn't see any small houses. It looked as if people lived together in the large buildings. Far in the future, there seemed to be no more families and no more homes.

I looked back and saw that a small group of Eloi had followed me on my walk. It was then that I noticed how much they all looked alike. They wore the same clothes. They wore their hair the same. They had the same thin bodies. From a distance, it was hard to tell the men and women apart. The only difference between the children and adults was their size. Most of the things that make us different were gone.

Soon, I was alone at the top of the small hill. The climb was too hard for the Eloi, so they had left me. I found a yellow metal bench and sat down to look out at the countryside. The sun had set, and the sky was full of beautiful purples and reds. The colorful sky was reflected in the Thames as it curved into the distance.

From where I sat, it looked as if the great city of London had disappeared. There were no longer streets crowded with people and traffic. There wasn't row after row of homes, offices, shops, and factories. Instead, statues and tall buildings were spread out across the countryside. They dotted a lush, green landscape of grass, bushes, and trees for as far as the eye could see.

I didn't see any farms, either. There were no cattle or sheep to be seen in any of the fields.

There were no fields of grains or vegetables. It was as if the whole earth had become one endless garden.

I sat and thought about the future I had discovered. It seemed as if the world had become a paradise. No one appeared to work, and yet everyone had plenty to eat. There weren't any factories or machines, and yet everyone had clothes to wear and a place to live. I couldn't imagine the Eloi fighting or killing one another. My guess was that war was a thing of the past.

Even the weather seemed perfect. In the last moment before the Time Machine had come to a halt in the future, I had noticed that the country-side was green even in the winter. I wouldn't have been surprised if the Eloi wore their robes and sandals all year long.

As I sat on the bench, I noticed that the air was free of insect pests, and filled with colorful butterflies. I didn't see any weeds or harmful plants, but fruit trees and beautiful flowers were everywhere.

Below me, the Eloi strolled through their paradise. They all seemed healthy and happy. No one appeared to be richer or poorer than anyone else. For as far as I could see, there was no dirty air or water in sight. The world truly was a paradise.

As the sky darkened, I imagined how it had happened. Today, science is always making new discoveries that make our lives easier. We are finding better ways to fight illness. We invent new machines to do our work for us. We build machines that can travel across the oceans or fly through the air.

A couple of hundred years ago, there was no electricity. We hadn't invented the telegraph, steam engines, or railways yet. Now, only two centuries later, we have all those things.

Two hundred years ago, disease, war, and poverty were much worse than today. In such a short time, we have made great strides. Today, those problems cause less suffering than ever.

We have come so far in just two centuries. Imagine how far we could progress in hundreds of thousands of years.

Here, it was as if all the struggles and hardships of life had ended. The world of the future was a world without war, poverty, or illness. It was the world humans had always dreamed of. After eight hundred thousand years, the dream had come true.

At least, the dream had come true in some ways, I thought. In other ways, the Eloi and the world of the future disturbed me. Life was *too* easy. The Eloi did nothing but eat, sleep, laugh, and sing. Because of this, they'd become small and weak. They couldn't climb even a small hill—or else they were too lazy to be bothered.

And because they had everything they needed, they didn't have to use their minds, either. They didn't invent or build things anymore. They'd stopped making art and music. They'd left all these things in the past because they didn't need them anymore. Their bodies and their minds had become weak.

This bothered me. I had always imagined that humans would become more advanced as time passed. I thought we would grow smarter and our progress would never end. Instead, we'd turned into the Eloi. We'd become weak and simple, and spent all our days playing and eating fruit. It may sound like an enjoyable life, but to me it was the end of our growth as a race.

As I sat on the bench and looked out at the night, I felt disappointment at the world of the future. I didn't know then that there was even more to discover about this new world.

CHAPTER 6

The Disappearance
of the Time Machine

∽

The full moon was rising above the green countryside. The Eloi had gone. It was getting cold, so
I decided to walk down the hill and find a place to
sleep.

I looked back toward the white building where
I had eaten and saw the White Sphinx. Near it
were the bushes with purple flowers and the
grass lawn. Suddenly, I realized that something
was wrong. The lawn was empty. The Time
Machine was gone!

All at once, I imagined being trapped in the

future. What had happened to my machine? What if I couldn't return home? My heart filled with fear, and I ran down the hill as fast as I could. I ran so quickly that I tripped and fell, cutting my face. As I bolted through the bushes, I told myself that the Eloi must have moved it. Maybe they had pushed it into the bushes where I couldn't see it, or moved it into one of their buildings. But deep down, I knew it wasn't them. They hadn't shown any interest in the machine when I arrived. And besides, they weren't strong enough to move it. Something else must have happened to it. Why had I left the machine?

Finally, I reached the lawn. I searched for my invention in the bushes, but I found nothing. I pulled at my hair and looked up. The Sphinx seemed to look down at me with a laughing smile on its face.

I didn't know who had moved the Time Machine or where it was, but at least I knew that it hadn't been sent through time. I still had the lever in my pocket, and the machine would not work without it. But where could it be?

I was filled with panic again. I ran through the bushes in the moonlight. As I dashed about, I scared some sort of white animal and it ran off. I guessed that it was a deer. Finally, I gave up and returned to the great white building. The hall where I had eaten was empty. I lit a match and wandered into the next room.

The floor of the room was covered with cushions. The Eloi were lying on them, asleep. Some woke up and looked at me. I grabbed them by the shoulders and shook them. "Where is my Time Machine?" I cried. Some laughed, and some were confused at my question. I finally stopped when I saw how foolish I was acting.

I ran out of the room and into the moonlight. I could hear the Eloi yelling from inside the building. They sounded frightened. It was as if they didn't want me to go outside.

I was very tired and upset, but I tried to look for my machine again. As I stumbled through the bushes, I thought I saw more animals hiding in the shadows. Finally, I couldn't search anymore. I lay down on the ground near the Sphinx and quickly fell asleep.

When I woke up, it was morning. I sat up and remembered my problem. But the sun was shining and I was rested. Last night's panic was behind me, and I felt better.

Instead of running around in the bushes, I knew I would have to learn more about this world. If the Time Machine was gone, maybe

I could find enough tools and parts to make another. If I couldn't, at least this world was beautiful and carefree. I could be happy here.

But my best hope was still to search for my machine. I began by asking the Eloi if they knew where it was. But they didn't understand my questions, and I got nowhere.

So I carefully examined the lawn. It wasn't long before I found a mark in the grass where something had been dragged. I also came across small, oddly shaped footprints. The mark and the footprints led me to the base of the White Sphinx.

The base was made of bronze and had square panels on its sides. They didn't have handles, but I was sure the panels were doors. I knocked on the doors. From the sound, I could tell the base was hollow. It was clear to me that my Time Machine was inside the base of the statue, behind the bronze doors. How it got there was another question.

Two young Eloi in orange robes were watching me. I smiled at them and motioned to them to come closer. I showed them that I wanted to open the bronze doors. It was clear from the looks on their faces that this idea bothered them very much. It was as if I had said something rude and shocking. They turned and walked away, mumbling to each other as they looked back over their shoulders.

I tried again with another fellow, but he acted the same way. As he walked away, I lost my temper. I ran after him, grabbed his robe, and pulled him back toward the Sphinx. But his face filled with horror and fear, and I let him go.

If I was going to get inside the base, I would have to do it alone. I banged my fist on the metal door. It was very odd, but I thought I heard a sound like a laughing voice. I found a big rock on the ground nearby and hammered the base until

I had put a dent in it. But my effort did nothing to help get me inside.

I was hot and tired, so I left the statue and headed to the hill again. I sat on the metal bench and thought about my problem. I realized that I just had to stay calm and take my time. I wasn't going to get my machine back by banging on the metal walls. If they had it—whoever *they* were!—I needed to wait and find out more about them. Again, I saw that I needed to learn more about this world. I had to find clues that would help me recover my Time Machine.

CHAPTER 7

More Discoveries

Once I had calmed down, my problem seemed funny. I thought about how hard I had worked to travel to the future—and now all I wanted to do was go home! I shook my head and laughed out loud.

When I returned to the white building, I felt as if the little people were staying away from me. Maybe it was because I had tried to get into the statue—or maybe it was just my imagination.

But after a day or two, things went back to normal. The Eloi were friendly again, and I tried to learn more of their language. It seemed to me that the little people used very few words. I learned the names of different fruits and how to say things like *run* or *hungry*. But that was all. Their sentences were also very short, with only one or two words. Because of this, I found it difficult to talk about anything but the simplest things.

I explored the countryside and tried not to think about the Time Machine too much. Everywhere I hiked, I saw the same gardens, grass, flowers, fruit, statues, and buildings.

I also saw more of the wells that I had seen before. There were many of them, and they seemed to be very deep. They were all made of metal and had small roofs to keep out the rain. I couldn't see any water when I looked down them, but I could hear a sound coming from below—a steady *thud-thud-thud,* like the sound of a big engine. I discovered that air was flowing down into all of them. I tossed a scrap of paper into one, and it was sucked quickly out of sight into the darkness.

I also discovered what I would describe as chimneys near each well. At the top of each chimney, the air shimmered. It looked as if hot air was coming out of them. I decided that fresh air must flow underground through the wells, and bad air must rise to the surface by way of the chimneys. But I had no idea why.

It reminded me how little I knew about the world of the future. Yes, I had met the Eloi and eaten their food. And I now slept with them in the white building. I'd discovered the wells and chimneys. But there was so much I didn't know. I was really only guessing at what the world of the future was truly like.

It was the same as if a caveman visited London. He would see buildings and cars. He would eat our food. But he wouldn't really know how anything worked. The railway, factories, telephones, and radios would all be a mystery. He wouldn't understand why we live the way we do. That's how I felt. And that's why I can say *what* I saw. But I can't say anything more than that.

For example, I never saw any graveyards. Why? Perhaps they were in another part of the country, or I just hadn't seen one in my travels. I don't know. I also never saw any sick or old people. Again, I don't know why.

I also began to wonder how the fruit got from tree to table. I never saw the Eloi pick any. I wondered where their robes and sandals came from. I never saw any factories where clothing or shoes could be made. Someone must be making these things, but where? There were no shops that sold food or clothing, and no boats or trains to carry goods. The little people spent all their time playing, or bathing in the river, or eating and sleeping. I could not imagine how things got done.

There was so much I didn't know about this world. Who had taken the Time Machine—and why? What were the wells and chimneys for? I had spent three days in the future, and there were so many questions I still needed to answer.

CHAPTER 8

Weena

∽

So the world was a mystery. But at least I was able to make a friend. On the third day of my stay, I was watching some of the Eloi bathing and playing in the river. One got caught in the faster part of the river and started to drift downstream. None of the Eloi did anything. They just watched as their friend cried for help and was carried farther away. So I quickly waded into the river and grabbed the young Eloi's arm. I could see now that it was a young woman. I pulled her to shore, carried her to a shady spot, and gently laid her down on the grass. After a few minutes, she felt better and I left her alone.

Later that day, I was returning from a hike. Suddenly, the same young woman appeared carrying handfuls of flowers. She laughed with delight and handed me the gift. I had been feeling lonely since arriving in the future. It made me feel good to see her smile and to receive the flowers from her. We sat on a bench and talked as best we could. I discovered that her name was Weena.

From that day, she followed me everywhere. She even tried to come with me on my hikes. But I needed to explore the countryside, and I wasn't sure she would be able to keep up, so I made her stay at home. When I did this, she became very upset. But we both felt happy when I returned at the end of the day. It made me feel like I was coming home.

I soon discovered that Weena and the Eloi were afraid of the dark. They were happy and carefree during the day, but when night fell, the little people hurried into their great buildings. I never saw one outside after sunset.

I also discovered that they never slept alone. In fact, they became quite upset when I slept in a small room by myself. I also noticed that if I entered one of these large sleeping rooms at night without a light, they became frantic.

One morning, I dreamed that I was drowning and that sea creatures were crawling over my face. I woke up suddenly and thought I saw an animal run from my room. I couldn't fall back to sleep again, so I got up and stepped outside for some fresh air. I stood at the top of the front stairs and looked out at the countryside.

The moon was setting. The dawn light was dim, and the bushes were still very dark. I looked at a nearby hill and, to my surprise, saw some animals running about. They looked like large apes, and were as white as ghosts. When they disappeared into the bushes, I wondered if I'd really seen them or if it was my imagination.

As the sun rose and the light got brighter, I looked for the creatures again. But they were gone. *Maybe they were ghosts,* I said to myself as a joke. I laughed. But inside, I was worried about these new beings.

CHAPTER 9

Encounter with a Ghost

∽

Later that same morning, I went on another hike. It was very early, but the morning was already hot. The world of the future was much warmer than the world of today. Maybe it was because the sun had grown hotter. Or maybe the earth was closer to the sun. Whatever the reason, it was so hot that I went in search of some cool shelter.

I came to a large building that had started to fall apart and climbed in through a hole in one wall. Inside, I found a hallway. It was very dark because the windows were blocked with broken stone and metal.

Suddenly, I stopped. A pair of glowing eyes looked out at me from the dark shadows. The eyes made me think of the creature I had seen in the bushes and the ghost-like animals on the hill.

I wanted to run, but I managed to stay calm. Instead of fleeing, I took a step forward and said, "Who's there?" I slowly walked closer. I put out my hand and felt something soft. I gasped as something ran past me from the shadow. It was a strange, ape-like creature. It ran into the light behind me with its head down. It must have had its eyes closed, too, because it ran into a wall and stumbled. The thing got up quickly and darted into the shadows behind a pile of rubble.

I didn't get a good look at it, but I knew it was covered in white hair and had large, grayish-pink eyes. Still, I couldn't tell if it ran on four legs or whether it used its arms to help itself run.

Fighting my fear, I followed it into the shadows. I couldn't see it anywhere. It was as if it had disappeared. As I searched the darkness, I found a well—just like the ones I had seen outside. I wondered if the thing had climbed down into it. I lit a match and peered over the edge. There it was, looking up at me with its shining eyes. It clung to a twisted metal ladder that wound its way down the side of the well. The thing looked like a human spider as it clambered down from rung to rung. Then the match burned my finger, and I dropped it. By the time I'd lit another, the creature was gone.

I sat staring into the inky darkness for a long time. As I peered down the well, I realized that the thing wasn't some kind of animal. It was covered in hair and moved like an ape. But when I saw its face, I knew it wasn't a wild creature. It had to be human. In an instant, everything I had thought about the world of the future changed.

I now saw that there were two kinds of humans. There were the gentle little people who lived in the Upperworld, and there were the ape-like humans who lived underground and did not like the bright light of day.

Just then, two Eloi ran into the hallway. They became upset when they saw me looking down the well. I tried to ask them a question, but they were frightened and turned to go.

I lit a match to see down the well. At the sight of the flame, the two Eloi stopped. They approached me and stood looking at the match. Their eyes widened, and they smiled with delight. It was as if they were seeing the most beautiful sight ever. The Eloi had probably forgotten how to make fire long ago, and fires from lightning would be very rare. So the sight of a flame was magical to them.

As they stared at the flickering match, I asked them another question about the well, but they didn't answer. And when the flame died, they left. So I went outside, too, and started to look for Weena.

My mind was spinning as I made my way to the white building. I thought I'd understood how the world had changed in eight hundred thousand years, but I had been wrong about so much. Now I saw that the ghost-like creatures lived underground. They had large eyes, just like owls or cats that prowl at night. With such large eyes, they found the sunlight too bright. That's why the thing had closed its eyes and run into the wall.

Their white hair reminded me of animals that live in caves and never see the sun. Those animals are often white, too.

I passed by another well. I'd already guessed that fresh air flowed down the wells and foul air came up through the chimneys. Now I knew why. The air was so these creatures could breathe. I saw the wells everywhere I went, so I knew there must be miles and miles of tunnels and caves beneath my feet.

This answered so many of my questions. The humans who lived underground must do all the work. They gathered the fruit at night and placed it on the tables while the Eloi slept. They also made the robes and sandals for the little people.

As a handful of Eloi began to walk with me, I wondered how the human race had become two races.

I started to think about the London I had left behind. I thought of the many people who spend most of their day belowground. There are people who work on the underground railways, and in the tunnels and sewers that run under the city. There are miners. And there are workers who toil in the depths of dark factories.

Every year, their numbers grow. We build more tunnels, dig deeper mines, and put more of our city belowground. Even today, many

Londoners spend most of their lives working, eating, and sleeping without seeing the sun.

And so, as the centuries passed, we must have put more of the city underground. More and more workers left the surface for lives in the Underworld.

Meanwhile, the educated and rich stayed aboveground. They built their parks and gardens and put up statues. They lived easy and simple lives while the people who lived underground did all the work.

As a white building appeared through the bushes, I imagined that this may have worked fine for a long time, but slowly the two groups had grown more and more different. By the time I arrived in the future, they had become two completely different races. The people of the Upperworld didn't work, so they became weak, lazy, and fearful. I didn't know very much about the creatures who lived below, but it was easy to see that they were turning into animals.

I learned that the Underworld creatures were called Morlocks. I was now sure that they had taken my Time Machine. But why? And if the Eloi were the masters, why couldn't the little people make the Morlocks return it to me?

Whenever I asked Weena these questions, she would get very upset. I don't know if she really understood what I was asking, but the word "Morlocks" frightened her. Once, she even cried. And so I stopped asking her about the things that puzzled me.

CHAPTER 10

A Visit to the Underworld

∼

Before I knew about the Morlocks, I thought the world was a peaceful place. Now that I knew the Eloi were not alone, I felt uneasy. Just like the Eloi, I began to fear the dark nights. I now knew that the Morlocks prowled the darkness, and the idea that these strange creatures roamed freely while I slept was very disturbing. I remembered waking with the feeling that an animal had disturbed me while I was asleep. I could understand why Weena and her people huddled together in large rooms at night.

I thought about my machine. It now seemed as if I could get it back by going underground to find it. If only I had someone to go with me— someone who was stronger and braver than the Eloi. The thought of climbing down one of the dark wells by myself frightened me.

But I was alone. So I told myself once more that the best thing for me to do would be to learn as much as I could about the Morlocks, the Eloi, and their world. Perhaps then I could figure out an easier way to recover my machine.

I began to take longer hikes to explore more of the countryside. On one of these walks, I saw a green building towering in the distance. It was larger than any building I had seen in the world of the future. I wanted to explore it, but it was getting late and I didn't want to be out at night.

So I returned home and told myself I would visit it tomorrow.

But by the next morning, I knew I didn't really need to visit the green building. Exploring it wouldn't help me find my Time Machine. It was just that the thought of climbing down a well frightened me terribly. The green building was just an excuse to stay aboveground.

No—what I really needed to do was visit the Underworld. And so I made up my mind to climb down into a well that morning.

I remembered seeing one nearby and I headed in that direction with Weena. She walked along happily until we reached the dark hole. When I leaned over the edge and looked down, she became very upset. I kissed her on the cheek and said, "Good-bye, little Weena."

Then I put one leg over the edge of the well. My little friend let out a cry and began pulling at my arm. I took her hands from my arm, grabbed hold of the side of the well, and put my other leg over the edge. I tried to make her feel better by giving her a smile. Then I grasped the metal ladder and lowered myself into the darkness.

The well was deep, and the climb down was difficult because the ladder was made for small hands and feet. One of the metal rungs bent when I stepped on it, and I almost fell into the blackness. I hung in the air by one hand until I recovered safely.

Down and down I went. My arms and back began to hurt, but I kept going. I looked up and saw a small blue circle of sky. I also saw Weena, staring down at me from high above.

The *thud-thud-thud* of a machine grew louder as I got farther from the surface. I was now very tired and in pain, and I didn't know how much farther I could go. I looked up again and saw that

Weena had gone. Then I looked around and saw a tunnel in the side of the well. I climbed into it and lay down for a much needed rest.

I don't know how long I lay in the tunnel, but suddenly I felt a soft hand on my face. I sat up quickly, found my matches, and lit one. In the light, I saw three Morlocks crouching in the tunnel looking at me. Their eyes were large and sparkled with the light of the match. Now that I saw them up close, I could see that they had sharp teeth. But the flame was too bright for them, and they quickly crawled into the shadows. I could still see their eyes staring at me from the dark.

I tried to talk to them, but their language must have been different from the Elois', and they didn't reply. I wanted to climb back up the well, but I knew I couldn't turn back now. So I lit another match and crawled down the tunnel. As

I made my way, the Morlocks stayed ahead of me, just beyond my small circle of light. Soon, I came to a large cavern. It was big, and the light of the match didn't reach the far wall.

In the cavern, I could just see the dark shapes of large machines. Morlocks crouched in the shadows, watching me. The air was stuffy and warm. The throbbing sound of the machines filled the air and echoed off the cavern walls.

Just then, my match flickered out. Right away I realized how helpless I was. I didn't have any of the things I needed to explore the Underworld safely. I only had a handful of matches left because I'd wasted some of them by showing fire to the Eloi. I hadn't brought any medicines or first-aid supplies with me from the past. I hadn't even thought to bring a camera! Instead, all I had with me in the tunnel were four matches.

In the darkness, I felt a hand brush against mine. Other hands grabbed at my clothes. Sharp claws dug into my skin. The creatures were so close, I could smell them and hear them breathing. I yelled loudly, and they backed away for a moment. Then they crawled toward me again. As their clawed fingers touched me, they made odd growling sounds. I shouted again, but this time they made a laughing sound in reply.

I lit another match and burned a small piece of paper I had in my pocket. The Morlocks backed away, and I retreated into the tunnel toward the well. But the burning paper quickly went out, and the creatures scrambled after me.

As I crawled toward the dim glow of the well, hairy hands grabbed me again and tried to drag me back into the cavern. I struck another match and waved it in their faces. They were so close, I could see their features clearly. Their large eyes were grayish-pink and had no eyelids. Their skin was pale, and they had no chins. I was terrified at the sight of them. If they weren't so afraid of the light, I don't know what they would have done to me.

When I lit the match, they let me go and I hurried down the tunnel. When it died, I lit another and was finally able to reach the well. As I grabbed for the ladder, the Morlocks clutched at my leg. I lit my last match, but the air flowing from the surface quickly blew it out. I grabbed a rung and kicked at the creatures with my feet. They let go, and I quickly pulled myself into the shaft. As I scrambled up toward the surface, one of the Morlocks followed. He grabbed my foot and pulled my boot off. He stopped climbing after me only when the light from above became too bright.

I was so tired and frightened, I barely made it to the surface. I felt sick and had trouble holding on to the ladder. But at last I reached the

Upperworld and pulled myself over the edge of the well into the bright sunlight. I fell to the ground. Even the dirt smelled good to me. I remember Weena and the other Eloi gathering around me—and then I fainted.

CHAPTER 11

To the Green Building

～დ

After my narrow escape, I felt more helpless than ever. Before I went underground, I was hopeful I would find my machine and return to my own time. But now I saw that the Morlocks were standing in my way. And I saw that they were more like wild animals than humans. It wouldn't be easy to get the Time Machine back.

It sounds odd, but I also began to fear the new moon. That's when the nights are darkest and the Morlocks can roam freely without any light to bother them. I didn't know what they would do under the cover of complete darkness. I realized that as I became more afraid of the black of night, I was becoming more and more like the Eloi.

Something else had changed, too. Before I saw the Underworld, I thought the Eloi were like the rich people of our time. I thought they had an easy life with no worries. I imagined the Morlocks led unhappy lives and took care of the people on the surface.

But I saw that it wasn't as simple as that. Yes, the Morlocks lived in the dirt and darkness of the Underworld. And, if my guess was correct, they made clothing for the Eloi and fed them.

But I began to think that they served the Eloi simply because they'd done it for thousands of years. They couldn't stop any more than a bird could stop flying or a fish could stop swimming.

At the same time, they had become wild animals and probably attacked the Eloi when they had a chance. After all, they were ready to attack me, and I was much bigger and stronger than an Eloi. That's why the little people were so afraid of them. Now I understood why they were so fearful of the wells.

The Eloi had easy lives. They didn't have to work for food or shelter. But they had become weak and dull because they had been taken care of for thousands of years. The gentle Upper-worlders couldn't do anything for themselves. They were afraid of the night and were too weak to defend themselves against the Morlocks.

In some ways, *they* were like animals. They fled into their buildings at night, and they slept together because they were afraid.

At first, I thought the Eloi were the masters of the Morlocks. Now it seemed that the Morlocks were the masters of the Eloi.

But I was not like the Eloi. I was strong enough to fight the creatures. I was afraid—but I wouldn't let fear keep me from finding my machine. I would do what I had to do to survive in this world and return to my own time.

The first thing I did was make sure I was safe while I slept. The creatures had probably crept over me at night while I lay in bed, and the thought made me shudder. So I went looking for a building that would be safe. My search was useless. The Morlocks could easily break into any building I saw. I even thought of building some sort of tree house. But after seeing one Morlock climb down the well, I guessed that they were very good climbers. So I gave up on that idea.

Then I thought of the green building I'd seen on one of my hikes. Perhaps it could be my new home. So I set off with Weena at my side.

As we walked, Weena happily picked flowers. The pockets of my clothing always puzzled her, but she must have decided that they were for holding flowers because she filled them with beautiful blossoms.

The green building was farther than I remembered. Also, I was moving slowly because I was walking in bare feet. I had thrown away my one shoe earlier that day. It was already sunset when we finally saw the green towers in the distance.

Weena was tired and wanted to return to the safety of the white building. I pointed to the green building and tried to make her understand that we would be safer in our new home. I could tell she was worried, but she followed me, anyway.

The night was clear and still. As we walked, I wondered what the Morlocks thought of my visit. Did they think I was attacking them? I looked at the ground and imagined their tunnels and caverns beneath my feet.

Twilight turned into night. The sky became a dark blue. Stars began to appear, and the trees around us faded to black. Weena was very tired, and the darker it got, the more frightened she became. We walked into a small valley and came to a stream. I picked her up in my arms and waded across. As I carried her up the other side of valley, we passed some statues and buildings. I didn't see any Morlocks, but it was still early and the darkest part of the night lay ahead.

We climbed out of the valley and came to a thick black forest. I didn't like the idea of wandering through it in the darkness. It would have been hard enough to find our way through the thick tangle of trees and bushes in the daylight. I was very tired, too, so I decided we would sleep in the open, at the top of a hill on the edge of the forest.

Weena had fallen asleep in my arms, so I wrapped her in my jacket and gently put her on the grass. I sat beside her and kept watch as the night got darker. It was a clear evening, and the stars were a welcome and friendly sight. It was then that I noticed the constellations had changed. After hundreds of thousands of years, the stars had moved into new patterns in the sky. There was also a very bright red star I did not recognize. But the Milky Way looked the same. It was a soft band of light stretching across the sky. And Venus glowed brightly in the west like an old familiar friend.

Looking at the stars, I thought about the great distance I had traveled through time. Even though I had come eight hundred thousand years, I thought about how much further time stretched into the past and the future. It made me think that the world I knew was nothing. All our cities, countries, languages, books, music—they were all gone. They had been replaced by awful creatures who lived underground and frightened little people who lived above.

The hillside was quiet. Once or twice, I thought I saw something moving in the trees.

But I tried not to think about the Morlocks. Instead, I gazed at the sky and looked for any constellations that hadn't changed. I dozed off once or twice until, finally, the sky in the east grew brighter. The light became pink and warm. As the night faded, I felt hopeful that everything would be fine.

I woke Weena, and we hiked down the hill. During the night the forest had been dark and frightening. In the morning it seemed green and fresh. Weena and I found some fruit for breakfast. Soon, other Eloi appeared and everything seemed fine.

And so I began to feel even better, and thought about everything I needed to do. I still had to find a safe place to sleep. I also needed a torch so that I could return to the Underworld. A torch would give me light to see and would protect me from the Morlocks.

And I needed some kind of tool to help me break into the base of the White Sphinx. With fire and tools, I was confident I could recover my Time Machine. As we walked through the forest toward the towering green building, I decided that I would bring Weena with me to my own time. I had only known her a few days, but I was already growing very fond of my companion.

CHAPTER 12

The Museum

⌐∽

When we reached the green building, we found that it was empty and run down. There was broken glass in many of the windows, and the walls were cracked and in need of repair. On one of the walls, I saw what looked like writing. I asked Weena if she could read it, but the symbols meant nothing to her. Along with so many other things, the Eloi had forgotten how to read and write.

At the top of the tall staircase that led into the building, I turned and looked out over the countryside. I could still see the River Thames, but I was surprised to see another large river where there isn't one today. As my eyes followed the rivers in the direction of the ocean, I wondered what had happened to all the living things in the sea.

I turned and walked through the gaping front doors. Inside, we found ourselves in a very large, long room. It reminded me of a gallery in a museum. The floor was covered in a thick layer of dust that softened the sound of our footsteps. There was an odd collection of objects in the room and they, too, were covered in dust. In the center of the hall was part of an enormous skeleton about the size of an elephant. It looked like the remains of a giant sloth. The skull and upper bones were scattered on the floor. Other bones were worn away where rainwater had leaked through a hole in the roof.

At the other end of the gallery was the huge skeleton of a brontosaurus. The bones of the great dinosaur's long tail and neck stretched across the entire room.

As we walked through the gallery, it was clear that this was a museum. Ancient objects filled dust-covered glass cases around us. The room was brimming with a wonderful collection of fossils that had survived all these years.

The museum was huge, and I realized there must be many more rooms. It occurred to me that there might be displays that explained the history of the last eight hundred thousand years. There might even be a library! Those rooms would tell me so much more than a roomful of dinosaur bones. And so I took Weena's hand and went in search of more galleries.

We came to a room filled with displays that had been destroyed by the passage of time. It looked like the cases had once contained stuffed animals, but now there was nothing inside except dust and small pieces of fur or skin. I was sad to see the empty cases. Seeing an animal that I recognized would have been like seeing a friendly face.

The next gallery was the largest yet. It was long, and the floor sloped down away from us. Large white globes hung from the ceiling. They looked like lamps, but many of them were broken and there was no electricity. There were very few windows, too, so the room was quite dark.

The gallery was filled with large machines. They were rusted and falling apart. But being an inventor, I was excited to see them. I walked eagerly from one to the next. What did they do, I wondered? Perhaps one of them still worked. Perhaps one of them would help me overcome the Morlocks.

Suddenly, Weena clutched my arm and pulled herself close to me. I looked around and noticed we were now at the end of the hall. There were no windows in this part of the gallery, and the shadows were pitch black. Weena was afraid and hid her face in my chest.

My small friend's fear reminded me of my real reason for visiting the green building. I was supposed to be looking for shelter. Instead, I'd been wandering from gallery to gallery as if I were on vacation. I was so eager to explore the museum that I had forgotten everything else. It was late afternoon, and I was no closer to finding a safe place to sleep or tools to help me get my machine back.

So I turned to leave the darkened gallery. Just then, a soft, scuffling sound came from a shadowy corner of the room. I stopped and peered into the blackness. The dusty floor was covered with small footprints.

I glanced around at the machines near me. A

number of metal levers stuck out from one. The machine was rusted and falling apart. I grabbed a lever and pulled it off easily. I now had a weapon with which to defend myself. I took Weena by the hand, and we left the gallery, keeping a careful watch behind us.

The next room was even larger, with walls lined with shelves. Torn brown rags hung from the shelves. These tatters must have been the remains of books. The books had fallen apart long ago, and now there wasn't a single page left. It made me sad to think of all the history, stories, and ideas that had been lost. I imagined all the knowledge and beauty that used to be on those pages. And now they were nothing but dust.

We continued on until we came to a hall of chemistry. There were no holes in the walls or ceiling, and everything in the room was undisturbed.

I thought I might find something useful here, so I went from case to case with excitement. At last, I found a box of matches in one of them. I smashed the glass and pulled out the precious find. I tried one and was delighted to see that it worked. With light and fire to protect me from the Morlocks, I could now return to the Underworld. I turned to Weena with a big smile. I was so happy, I raised my arms in the air and danced around her.

I looked into more cases and found an odd-looking sealed jar. I opened it and found that it was full of something that felt like wax. From its smell, I could tell that it was a substance called camphor. I knew that camphor burned, so I formed a ball of it and put it in my pocket.

I searched the rest of the gallery in the hopes of finding explosives that I could use to get into the base of the Sphinx, but there were none. Still, I had the metal lever, which I thought I could use to pry open the metal doors. And I had the matches and camphor. I left the room feeling very happy.

Weena and I walked through gallery after gallery, but I didn't find anything else of use. The rooms were silent and dusty. Many of them were in ruin. One was filled with statues and carvings from around the world.

Another was made to look like a mine. It was here I found a display containing two sticks of dynamite! I shouted out loud with joy and smashed the case. With these, I could blast my way into the base and recover my machine.

Then I thought it would be a good idea to test them. I took a match and tried lighting one of the fuses. It wouldn't burn. I took a closer look at the dynamite. To my great disappointment, I saw that the sticks were not real. They had been made for display and were useless.

It was probably a good thing they were fake. If not, I think I would have run straight to the Sphinx. I would have lit the dynamite and blown up the statue. And I probably would have destroyed my Time Machine in the explosion.

We walked through more of the museum, but I didn't find one room that I thought would be safe at night.

After a while, Weena and I found our way outside. We picked some fruit and ate hungrily. Afterward we felt rested and refreshed. It was almost evening, and I thought about what to do next.

I was more sure than ever that I could break into the base of the statue using the metal lever. If we left right away, we could walk until it became dark. Then we could sleep outside and hike the rest of the way the next day. We would reach the White Sphinx early the next morning.

It would mean spending the night in the open, but I wasn't worried about that anymore. I had the one thing that would keep us safe from the Morlocks: fire.

CHAPTER 13

The Forest at Night

∽

With the daylight disappearing, we headed back. As we walked, Weena and I gathered firewood. We were both tired, and carrying the wood slowed us down, so we didn't get as far as I'd hoped. By the time we reached the forest, it was already night.

Weena didn't want to go through the woods in the dark. If I had been thinking straight, we would have stopped and built a fire. But I was very tired because I had not slept the night before, so I decided to carry on. I thought the forest was less than a mile wide and I was anxious to make it through to the other side as soon as possible.

I was sure the matches and camphor would get us through the forest safely. And I felt it would be better to make camp on the hill on the other side. I had also seen three dark figures hiding in the nearby shadows, and I wanted to get away from them.

But now I was faced with a problem. I knew I would need to light matches to keep the Morlocks away in the darkness of the forest. But that would be difficult if I was carrying the firewood and my metal lever.

So I decided to leave behind the sticks and branches I had collected. I dropped my firewood and turned to go. That was when I had an idea. I thought if I lit a fire, it would keep the Morlocks from following us. To be honest, I think I also wanted to frighten them because I had grown to hate the creatures.

I lit the pile of wood, and soon a large blaze lit up the trees and bushes around us. Weena was thrilled by the flames. She put her firewood on the ground and danced around with wide-eyed delight. She moved so close to the flames that she would have burned herself if I hadn't grabbed her.

I gestured to her to pick up her firewood again. Then I took her hand, and together we walked into the forest. For a little while the light from the blaze lit our way. I looked back and saw that the fire was spreading. Some bushes were now burning, and flames were creeping up the hill. I laughed at the thought of the Morlocks running away in fear.

Weena and I turned and headed deeper into the gloom of the forest. The glow from the fire

became dimmer until the only light came from dim patches of sky overhead. There was barely enough light to see the trail. I would have struck a match to light our way, but Weena had become too tired. She dropped the wood she was holding, and I had to carry her. I held her in one arm and the metal lever in the other.

For a while, the only sounds were the cracking of twigs under our feet and the whisper of our breathing. But then I heard rustling noises behind us. Slowly, the sounds drew closer and closer. I began to hear the animal noises of the Morlocks.

I felt a tug at my jacket. Then something pulled at my arm. Weena gave out a small cry. I could feel her shaking with fear.

I needed to light a match, so I put Weena down and reached into my pocket. As I was fumbling for a match, I heard the sound of a struggle beside me in the darkness. The Morlocks were trying to drag Weena away.

Small hands clutched at my jacket, and at my back and neck. I finally struck a match. It burst into flame, and in the light I saw the white, hairy backs of the Morlocks as they scrambled away. I quickly took the camphor from my pocket. I picked off a small piece, lit it, and threw it on the ground. It sparked and burned, driving the creatures even farther into the shadows. The rustle of the bushes and the glimmer of eyes in the darkness told me that the Morlocks were all around us.

I looked down and saw poor Weena. She was curled up on the ground, covering her head with her arms. I bent down and picked her up. I turned to go and suddenly realized I didn't know which direction to take. In my struggle with the Morlocks, the creatures had turned me around.

In the darkness, I didn't have any idea which way led back to the statue. For all I knew, I was facing back toward the green building. I began to sweat and tried to decide what to do.

I quickly realized we would have to camp here for the night. If we tried to go on, we could get hopelessly lost. The camphor was flickering out, so I began to gather wood for a fire. The Morlocks watched me from a distance. Their eyes shone like the eyes of wild animals in the blackness.

The camphor went out, and everything went dark. I quickly lit a match and saw two of the white creatures already creeping toward Weena. The light of the match blinded them, and they scurried away in a panic. One bolted with its eyes closed and ran right into me. It gave a yell and scrambled into the bushes. I rapidly lit another piece of camphor and gathered more firewood. Soon we were safely in a circle of light from the fire.

I needed to be ready if the Morlocks came again, so I placed the lever, the camphor, and the matches on the ground next to me. I dumped the matches out of their box so I could light them at a moment's notice.

I was already exhausted from the day, and the crackle of the burning wood made me even sleepier. I thought the fire would burn for another hour. And so, with Weena lying beside me, I closed my eyes to rest.

When I opened them again, I was in complete darkness and in the grips of the Morlocks. Their hands pawed me everywhere—grabbing my neck, hair, and arms. I tried to get up, but they pulled me down and held me to the ground. I felt teeth nipping at my body. I knew I must have slept too long. The fire had gone out, and the creatures had returned.

It was horrible to feel them on me. I felt like a fly trapped in a giant spiderweb. But I fought back and rolled over to knock them off me. I managed to free myself and scrambled to my feet. Now that I was standing, I could keep the Morlocks from grabbing me. They tried to jump on me, but I fought back and pushed them away. I stood with my back to a tree, which made it easier to defend myself.

It was then I noticed a faint glow creeping into the woods from behind me. As it grew brighter, the Morlocks stopped attacking and crept away. Then, more of the creatures appeared from the direction of the light. Their white backs shone a dull red as they fled. As I watched them hurry away, a glowing spark drifted by on the breeze. I heard a muffled roar behind me and took a deep breath—the air was filled with the smell of burning wood.

I stepped away from the tree and looked back. The dark forest had turned into a wall of flame.

The small blaze that I had started had turned into a huge forest fire. It lit up the trees and ground around me. I looked for Weena, but she was gone. The flames marched closer, filling the air with hissing and crackling sounds. Tree after tree burst into flame with a roar.

There was nothing to do but follow the Morlocks. I quickly grabbed the metal lever, camphor, and matches and ran. The fire raced through the forest almost as fast as I could run. But I stayed ahead of it until at last I came out into an open field.

The field was lit by the flames behind me. The fire reached the field, and soon trees, shrubs, and grass burned all around. At the top of a nearby hill, a bush was alive with flame.

Caught in the light, the Morlocks ran frantically from one side of the field to the other. They must have been running with their eyes closed, because they sometimes ran into one another or into trees. A few times, the creatures darted right at me and I had to jump aside.

I wasn't in any danger from the Morlocks while the fire burned, so I walked around looking for Weena. I covered every foot of the field, but she was nowhere to be seen.

Finally I gave up and fell to my knees on the hill. I felt as if I were in a nightmare. The flames and the ghostly figures of the frantic Morlocks surrounded me. I had lost my dear friend. And I had barely survived the attack in the forest.

I looked up. Through the billowing smoke, I saw that the sky was getting brighter. The stars were disappearing. The red glow of the fire was slowly being replaced by the pink light of dawn.

When the sun finally rose above the black-ened trees, I searched for Weena again. But she was still nowhere to be seen.

And so I left the hill and headed toward the white building in the distance. I was tired from the horrible night, but it wouldn't take me long to reach the statue.

Without Weena at my side, I felt more alone than ever.

CHAPTER 14

Recovering the Time Machine

∽

It wasn't long before I came to the yellow metal bench where I had sat on my first day in the future. Everything looked the same — the beautiful plants, the buildings, and the Eloi strolling quietly. Some of the little people were bathing in the river where I had saved Weena. Back then, I thought the Eloi lived a carefree life. The world had looked like a peaceful garden, free of fear or danger.

But from the bench I could also see the wells.

They reminded me of the Morlocks. I may have thought the world was a paradise, but I had been very wrong.

It made me sad to think that this was our future. For all of history, we have tried to make life better. We have tried to make the world a safer, more carefree place. And at some point in our future, we must have succeeded. I could see from the Eloi that we had conquered disease, war, and hunger. We had reached the goal we'd been working toward for thousands of years.

But this peaceful world only came about because half of humanity went underground to work. They said good-bye to the surface and the sun. They spent their lives in the dark, taking care of the people who stayed aboveground.

And the half who stayed on the surface? They had everything they needed. Everything was taken care of. So they grew weak and stopped using their brains. They had no more goals.

And so by the year eight hundred and two thousand, seven hundred and one, the Morlocks had turned into animals who did nothing but work, and the Eloi lived in fear of the dark.

I was exhausted, so I lay down on the grass and had a long sleep. When I woke up, I saw that I had slept for most of the day. The sun was setting, and the air was getting cool. I grabbed my metal lever and walked down the hill toward the White Sphinx. I reached into my pocket and made sure I still had some matches.

When I reached the Sphinx, I saw the most unexpected thing. The doors on the base of the statue were open. I carefully approached the door-way and looked in. There, sitting in the darkness, was my Time Machine. I wondered why the Morlocks were giving my machine back. Were

they giving up? Was I too strong for them? I dropped my metal lever and took another step toward the doorway.

Then another thought crossed my mind. Perhaps this was a trap. I laughed quietly to myself. If these creatures thought they were smarter than me, they were in for a surprise.

I stepped through the doorway and into the base of the statue. I walked up to my machine. It was good to see it again. I was thankful that it wasn't damaged.

But then, just as I had expected, the bronze doors quickly closed behind me. There was a loud *clang,* and I was suddenly in the dark. When the echoes of the slamming doors faded, I heard the murmur of the creatures coming toward me.

I wasn't afraid. This is what I had thought the Morlocks would do. All I had to do now was put the control lever in the machine and escape through time. I would disappear, and the Underworld creatures wouldn't know what had happened.

I reached into my pocket and pulled out a match. I struck it against a metal rail of the machine, but it did not light. I had made a terrible mistake. The match was the kind that would only light if you struck it on the matchbox, and I had left the box in the forest when I fled from the fire.

You can imagine how quickly my calm turned to panic. The Morlocks were all around me. I could feel them touching me. They grabbed at me and I pushed them away as best I could. I climbed into my machine and pulled the control lever from my pocket. Hairy hands grasped at me as I tried to pull myself into the seat. In the struggle, I dropped the lever to the ground. I reached down with one hand and found it in the dark. While the Morlocks tried to pull me from the machine, I put the lever in place.

As I lay sideways across the seat, I pushed the lever forward. The clutching hands slipped from me. A soft gray light appeared, and I felt myself traveling through time once more.

CHAPTER 15

Into the Future Again

Once again, I felt the strange sensation of hurtling into the future. I became dizzy, and my stomach was queasy. I had the feeling that I was falling. It was even worse this time, because I was sitting sideways in the seat. I hung on as the machine swayed and shook. Still, I was glad to be free from the clutches of the Morlocks. I had left them behind—not by running away from them, but by fleeing through time.

After a few minutes, I looked at the dials in front of me. The hand that showed the passing of thousands of days was sweeping around like the second hand of a watch. I was racing through time faster than ever.

I was speeding ahead so rapidly that the blinking of day and night turned into an even, gray light. But then, I was puzzled to see the flashing of day and night again. The sun should have been moving across the sky too fast for me to see it. But for some reason, I could see it moving from horizon to horizon. As I watched, it seemed to slow down. Then the sky grew dark, and the sun disappeared altogether. Moments later, it rose again.

I was surprised to see this. The dials did not show that I was slowing down. It was as if a single day had become thousands of years long.

Finally, the sky turned the color of twilight. Even though I was still traveling swiftly into the future, there was no more night and day. The sun sat motionless near the western horizon without rising or setting. It had also grown larger and redder. The moon had disappeared, and the stars shone, even though the sun had not set.

Then I realized what was happening. Today, the earth spins around on its axis once every day, so we see the sun and moon move through our sky once every twenty-four hours.

But far in the future, the spinning of the earth has slowed and days have become longer. I had reached a point in time when the turning of the planet had slowed to a complete stop. The earth did not spin, and the sun didn't rise or set.

I pulled back on the lever very carefully. The hands on the dials slowed until only one was turning—the dial showing the passing of single days. Slowly, the dim outline of a beach grew visible. I pulled the lever back all the way to its starting point and came to a halt.

I sat in the Time Machine and gazed out at the new world. To the east, the stars shone in a sky of inky blackness. Overhead, there were no stars and the heavens were a deep red. To the west, the sky was a brilliant scarlet, lit by the sun sitting on the horizon.

The ground around the Time Machine was covered with rocks that glowed red in the light. The only plant life was the green moss that covered the rocks.

Farther from the machine was a beach that sloped down to the sea. There wasn't a breath of wind, and there were no waves on the surface of the water. The only motion was the slow rise and fall of a gentle swell. A thick crust of salt ringed the water's edge.

I felt light-headed and noticed that I was having trouble breathing. I could tell that the air had grown thinner. It was like trying to breathe at the top of a tall mountain.

I looked up the beach and saw what looked

like a huge white butterfly. It darted about through the air and disappeared over a small hill.

Then I noticed something moving on the ground nearby. At first, I thought one of the large, flat rocks was moving. Then I saw that it was a giant crab, slowly crawling toward me. Its shell was as wide as a table, and it had many legs. As I watched, it unfolded two big claws from under its body and waved them in the air. The thing raised its long antennae and whipped them about. Its eyes were small black balls sitting on top of stems that stuck up from the shell. The crab's broad back was rough, like the surface of a rock, and was spotted with green moss. Its mouth was an opening near the front edge of the body. There were small pincers on either side of the mouth. The crab probably used those pincers to feed itself.

As I stared at the strange creature crawling toward me, I felt a tickling on my cheek. It felt like a fly, and I brushed it away with my hand. But then I felt another tickle on my ear. I waved at it with my hand and caught something that felt like a piece of string. The string quickly pulled itself from between my fingers. I turned and saw that it was the antenna of another giant crab, climbing up on the outside of the Time Machine. Its eyes wriggled in front of my face, and its mouth pincers moved hungrily. It reached toward me with one of its large, grasping claws.

I quickly grabbed the lever and sped a month into the future. Because the crab had been on the outside of the machine, it did not travel through time with me. When I came to a stop, it was gone. But dozens of other crabs crawled along the shoreline in the dim light.

As I sat looking at the bleak and barren world of the distant future, I felt a great sense of sadness. The red sky, the dead sea, the giant crabs, and the thin air—everything made me feel hopeless and alone.

After a few minutes, I pushed the lever and moved forward a hundred years. The red sun still sat near the horizon, but it seemed even larger and dimmer. The sea hadn't changed, and the beach remained alive with crabs. It was still hard to breathe. And in the western sky, a thin crescent moon hung over the sea.

I continued my journey through time, halting every thousand years or so. At every stop, the sun appeared larger and dimmer. I had read books on astronomy. I knew that as the sun grew older, it would turn into a giant red star. But I never imagined I would see it with my own eyes.

I stopped for a final time and saw from the dials that I was more than thirty million years in the future. The sun was now huge. The crabs had disappeared, and the moss was the only sign of life. The air was much cooler, and a light snowfall dusted the rocks. In the distance, I could see snow-covered hillsides. Along the shore, the white crust of salt was mixed with broken sheets of ice.

I looked out at the ocean and saw that a shallow sandbank had appeared above the oily surface of the water. As I watched, I thought I saw something move on the sandbank, but finally I decided it must have been a wave.

Then I noticed something odd about the sun. It looked as if a large, round object was moving in front of it. The black shadow slowly blocked more and more of the sun, and the sky began to dim. It was one of Earth's neighboring planets. It was much larger than I would have expected. The planets of the solar system must have moved much closer together after all these millions of years.

The world was perfectly silent. It's hard to describe to you just how quiet it was. There were no sounds of carriages, factories, or people. There were no bird songs, nor the hum of insects.

As the neighboring planet continued to block more of the sun's light, the silence was broken by the faint sound of a wind from the east. The snowfall grew heavier. The distant hills became lost in the growing darkness. Soon, it was as if night had fallen. The sky became black, and the stars appeared.

I began to shiver from the cold and was having trouble breathing. I thought I would feel warmer if I stretched and moved about, so I climbed out of the machine. The dark planet was moving away from the sun, but I still felt chilled.

As I stood beside my machine, I saw something stir on the sandbank again. This time, I could see that it was some kind of living creature. Its round, black body was the size of a football. It dragged itself along the sand by its tentacles.

127

I tried to fill my lungs with air, but I felt as if I was about to faint. The thought of lying helpless on the rocks filled me with terror, and I found the strength to climb back into my machine. I put my hand on the lever and pulled.

CHAPTER 16

The Time Traveler Returns

⌒

And so I began my journey back in time from the distant future. I sat in the seat and watched as the blinking of days and nights returned. The sun shone a brilliant white again. The sky became its familiar blue, and the ocean disappeared from view. Trees and grass appeared, and the countryside became green again.

The dials spun backward until the one showing millions of days stopped at zero. I was almost back to present day. I slowed my speed. Buildings rose up around me. The dial showing thousands of days reached zero, too. Then, the walls of my workshop appeared. Very gently, I slowed the Time Machine even more.

At one point, I saw everyone at the workshop door, looking into the room.

Then I saw my housekeeper again. She walked across the workshop in the blink of an eye—just as before. But because I was traveling backward through time, she was moving in reverse.

Then I stopped. I was in my old workshop again. It was good to see everything—my tools, workbenches, and drawings. It was good to hear the sound of traffic coming from outside. I took a deep breath and smelled the air that I knew so well.

I got out of the Time Machine. I was shaking and my legs were weak, so I sat down in a chair. I looked around. Everything was exactly the way I had left it. I almost wondered if I'd simply fallen asleep. Perhaps my adventure was nothing more than a dream.

But not everything was exactly the same. When I started my journey, the Time Machine was sitting in one corner of the workshop. But when I returned, it was sitting on the other side of the room. In the future, the Morlocks had dragged it from the lawn into the base of the statue. That meant that it had been moved from one side of the room to the other in the present.

I got up from the chair and walked into the hallway. There was a newspaper on the table by the front door. I looked at it and saw today's date. Then I looked at the clock and saw that it was almost eight o'clock in the evening.

That's when I heard your voices and the clatter of dishes in the dining room. At first, I just wanted to go upstairs because I was still feeling weak and sick. But then I smelled the meal. I opened the door and . . . well, you know the rest. I washed and ate, and now I am telling you my story.

CHAPTER 17

The Proof

∽

"I know that all of this must sound incredible to you," the Time Traveler said. "I don't expect you to believe me. You must think I'm lying, or making it all up."

"You could earn a living writing stories like this," the editor said with a sigh.

"So you don't believe me?" asked the Time Traveler. "I didn't think you would. I hardly believe it myself. But then, how do you explain these?"

We all watched as the Time Traveler reached into the pocket of his robe and pulled out two wilted flowers. He placed them on the table in front of us, and we all stared at them. They didn't look like any flower I knew. The Time Traveler looked down at them with a smile on his face, as if he was recalling a fond memory.

"They're the flowers that Weena put in my jacket pocket," he explained.

"The doctor got up from his chair to look more closely at the flowers our friend had taken from his pocket. "It's odd. I've never seen this type of flower before. May I have them?" he asked.

"Certainly not," answered the Time Traveler.

After a moment, the doctor asked, "Where did you really get them?"

The Time Traveler closed his eyes and rubbed his forehead with his hands. He took his hands away and opened his eyes. When he spoke, he sounded upset. "I got them from Weena."

Then he looked around the room. A look of doubt and confusion appeared on his face. "Or did I? Did I really travel through time? Or was it all a dream? Is there really a machine sitting in my workshop?"

He stood up quickly and grabbed the lamp from the table. He opened the door and rushed into the hallway. We all followed him as he made his way to the workshop.

The Time Machine sat in the corner of the room. We gathered around it. The metal, ivory, and crystal glimmered in the lamplight. I reached out and touched its metal frame. It looked the same as before—except for bits of grass, moss, and dirt on its frame. I also saw that a metal rail was slightly bent, just as the Time Traveler had described.

The Time Traveler put the lamp on the bench. He ran his fingers along the bent rail. Seeing the machine again seemed to make our friend feel better. It was as if the dirt and damage proved that his story was true. "It did happen, then. It's all true."

He picked up the lamp, and we followed him out into the hall. He seemed very tired, so we put on our coats to leave. The doctor shook the Time Traveler's hand and said, "You should rest. You've been working too hard." The Time Traveler laughed loudly and said good night.

After I left, I spent most of the night thinking about the fantastic tale. Could it be true? The Time Traveler had no reason to make up the story. And I had no reason not to believe him.

The next day, I happened to pass by his house. I decided to drop in and see how he was feeling after a good night's sleep. I knocked on the door and was greeted by the housekeeper. She told me the Time Traveler was in his workshop.

I walked down the hallway and entered the room, but he was not there. I stared at the Time Machine for a moment, and touched the lever. I tried to imagine it journeying through the ages.

When the Time Traveler did not appear after a few minutes, I left the room. I walked down the hall, where I found my friend coming down the stairs. He had a small camera under one arm and a knapsack under the other. A large smile filled his face and he said, "I'm very busy right now."

"Do you really travel through time?" was all I could think to ask.

"Yes," he replied calmly as he looked me in the eyes. "Yes, I do. And I'll prove it to you beyond any doubt. Wait here and I'll be back in half an hour—with all the specimens and proof I need!"

He smiled and disappeared down the hallway and into the workshop. So I sat down in a room off the hallway, took out my newspaper, and began to read. Just then, I remembered that I was supposed to meet another friend shortly. I got up and went to find the Time Traveler. I wanted to tell him I had to leave, but that I would be right back.

As I reached the door to the workshop, I heard odd noises coming from inside. A gust of wind whirled around me as I opened the door. The sound of the wind was followed by the crash of broken glass.

I stepped inside the workshop. The Time Traveler was not there. The Time Machine had not moved, but it had become a ghostly blur. I thought I saw someone sitting in it, but I couldn't be certain. The machine was slowly disappearing. And then it was gone.

I stood in silence, staring at the spot where the invention had been sitting. I didn't know what to think. I decided to wait, in the hopes of hearing another strange story and seeing my friend's photographs and specimens from the future.

But that was three years ago. The Time Traveler has not returned. And I'm afraid that now he never will.

Epilogue

⚓

I still wonder—will I see the Time Traveler again, or has he disappeared into the depths of time? Perhaps he has gone back to when humans lived in caves or, even farther, to a time when dinosaurs roamed the earth.

Perhaps he has returned to the future. Perhaps he has traveled to a time before the Eloi and Morlocks. He'd always spoken of a future in which there were no wars, hunger, or illness. He'd always hoped that humans would solve the problems we face today. Perhaps he found that future and is living there now.

I still have the two strange flowers that he brought back with him from his adventure. They're brown and wilted now, but they remind me of his story.

They remind me of something else, too. The Eloi may have been weak and fearful, but the flowers were a gift of thanks from Weena to my friend. The flowers tell me that the human heart is still filled with kindness and love——even in the distant future.

What Do *You* Think?
Questions for Discussion

∽

Have you ever been around a toddler who keeps asking the question "Why?" Does your teacher call on you in class with questions from your homework? Do your parents ask you questions about your day at the dinner table? We are always surrounded by questions that need a specific response. But is it possible to have a question with no right answer?

The following questions are about the book you just read. But this is not a quiz! They are designed to help you look at the people, places, and events in the story from different angles. These questions do not have specific answers. Instead, they might make you think of the story in a completely new way.

Think carefully about each question and enjoy discovering more about this classic story.

1. When he learns about the time machine, the artist suggests that you could travel back in time and see all of history. Where in time would you most like to travel?

2. How does the Time Traveler communicate with the Eloi? Have you ever tried to speak to someone who couldn't understand you?

3. How does the Time Traveler react when he sees that his time machine is missing? Who did you think took it? Has anyone ever taken something that belonged to you?

4. Why are the Eloi afraid of the Sphinx? Do you think they are right to worry? What scares you?

5. The Time Traveler realizes that humans evolved into two species because some people lived aboveground and others spent all their time belowground. Where would you prefer to live?

6. When the Time Traveler climbs down the well, he brings one "weapon"—matches. Knowing what he did about the Morlocks, do you think this was a wise decision? What would you have brought down the well?

7. The Time Traveler says that he decided to bring Weena back to his own time. Do you think this is a good idea? How do you think Weena would react to 1845?

8. What kinds of displays do Weena and the Time Traveler find in the museum? Which room would you most like to explore?

9. How do the Time Traveler's friends react to his story? Would you believe it if you were them? What is the strangest story anyone has ever told you?

10. What do you think the Time Traveler takes with him the second time he travels into the future? What would you take?

Afterword

By Arthur Pober, EdD

⌒

First impressions are important.

Whether we are meeting new people, going to new places, or picking up a book unknown to us, first impressions count for a lot. They can lead to warm, lasting memories or can make us shy away from any future encounters.

Can you recall your own first impressions and earliest memories of reading the classics?

Do you remember wading through pages and pages of text to prepare for an exam? Or were you the child who hid under the blanket to read with a flashlight, joining forces with Robin Hood to save Maid Marian? Do you remember only how long it took you to read a lengthy novel such as *Little Women*? Or did you become best friends with the March sisters?

Even for a gifted young reader, getting through long chapters with dense language can easily become overwhelming and can obscure the richness of the story and its characters. Reading an abridged, newly crafted version of a classic novel can be the gentle introduction a child needs to explore the characters and story-line without the frustration of difficult vocabulary and complex themes.

Reading an abridged version of a classic novel gives the young reader a sense of independence and the satisfaction of finishing a "grown-up" book. And when a child is engaged with and inspired by a classic story, the tone is set for further exploration of the story's themes, characters, history, and details. As a child's reading skills advance, the desire to tackle the original, unabridged version of the story will naturally emerge.

If made accessible to young readers, these stories can become invaluable tools for understanding themselves in the context of their families and social environments. This is why the Classic Starts series includes questions that stimulate discussion regarding the impact and social relevance of the characters and stories today. These questions can foster lively conversations between children and their parents or teachers. When we look at the issues, values, and standards of past times in terms of how we live now, we can appreciate literature's classic tales in a very personal and engaging way.

Share your love of reading the classics with a young child, and introduce an imaginary world real enough to last a lifetime.

Dr. Arthur Pober, EdD

Dr. Arthur Pober has spent more than twenty years in the fields of early childhood and gifted education. He is the former principal of one of the world's oldest laboratory schools for gifted youngsters, Hunter College Elementary School, and former Director of Magnet Schools for the Gifted and Talented for more than 25,000 youngsters in New York City.

Dr. Pober is a recognized authority in the areas of media and child protection and is currently the U.S. representative to the European Institute for the Media and European Advertising Standards Alliance.

Explore these wonderful stories in our
Classic Starts™ library.

20,000 Leagues Under the Sea
The Adventures of Huckleberry Finn
The Adventures of Robin Hood
The Adventures of Sherlock Holmes
The Adventures of Tom Sawyer
Alice in Wonderland & Through the Looking Glass
Animal Stories
Anne of Avonlea
Anne of Green Gables
Arabian Nights
Around the World in 80 Days
Ballet Stories
Black Beauty
The Call of the Wild
Dracula
The Five Little Peppers and How They Grew

Frankenstein

Great Expectations

Greek Myths

Grimm's Fairy Tales

Gulliver's Travels

Heidi

The Hunchback of Notre-Dame

Journey to the Center of the Earth

The Jungle Book

The Last of the Mohicans

Little Lord Fauntleroy

Little Men

A Little Princess

Little Women

The Man in the Iron Mask

Moby-Dick

The Odyssey

Oliver Twist

Peter Pan